PIRATES OF THE SOUTHERN SEAS

BY SAM MAGGS AND KENDRA WELLS

AMULET BOOKS
NEW YORK

HUGE THANKS TO KENDRA, FOR THEIR PARTNERSHIP; BLAIR, FOR ALL
HIS LOVE; MY PARENTS, FOR THEIR UNENDING SUPPORT; LUCIDITY
EDITORIAL, FOR THEIR SENSITIVITY READ; MARIA VICENTE AND
CHARLOTTE GREENBAUM, FOR BELIEVING IN US AND IN THE BOOK;
AND TO LITTLE EEVEE, FOR THE CUTENESS
— SAM MAGGS

TO MY COMICS PEERS WHO INSPIRED AND EMPOWERED ME, TO ALL
THE D&D SHOWS AND PODCASTS THAT KEPT ME COMPANY WHILE I
WORKED, TO MY THERAPIST FOR EVERYTHING, AND TO MY FRIENDS,
MY FAMILY, AND PAT FOR EVERYTHING ELSE
— KENDRA WELLS

Library of Congress Control Number 2019950077

Hardcover ISBN 978-1-4197-3966-8
Paperback ISBN 978-1-4197-3980-4

Text copyright © 2021 Sam Maggs
Illustrations copyright © 2021 Kendra Wells
Book design by Megan Kelchner

Printed and bound in China
10 9 8 7 6 5 4 3 2 1

Amulet Books are available at special discounts when purchased in
quantity for premiums and promotions as well as fundraising or
educational use. Special editions can also be created to specification. For
details, contact specialsales@abramsbooks.com or the address below.

Amulet Books® is a registered trademark of Harry N. Abrams, Inc.

ABRAMS The Art of Books
195 Broadway, New York, NY 10007
abramsbooks.com

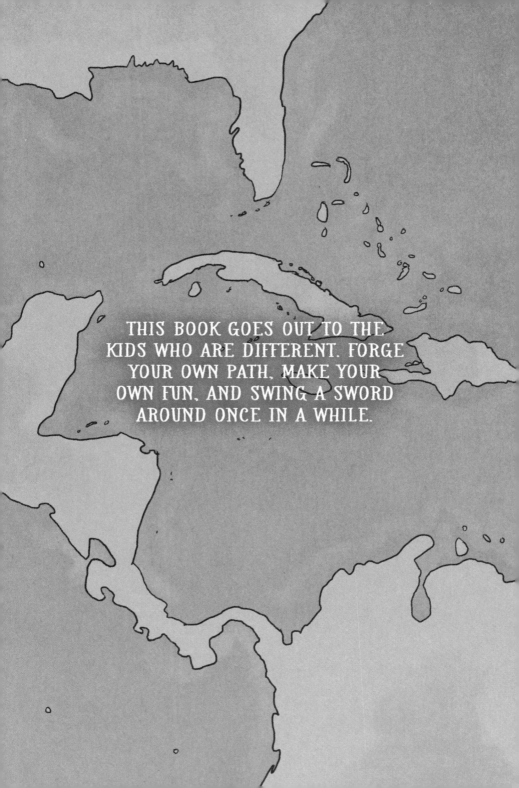

THIS BOOK GOES OUT TO THE
KIDS WHO ARE DIFFERENT. FORGE
YOUR OWN PATH, MAKE YOUR
OWN FUN, AND SWING A SWORD
AROUND ONCE IN A WHILE.

6

I JUST THINK WE SHOULD TRY IT *MY* WAY FOR ONCE.

OH, THE BORIN' WAY, THEN?

THE *STEALTHY* WAY.

THOSE THINGS ARE NOT TOYS, KATI!

THINGS THAT ARE FUN ARE TOYS. BY DEFINITION.

I STILL THINK WE'RE GOING TO GET SUNK.

HAVE YOU SEEN THE SIZE OF THAT SLOOP?

WHAT DOES THE *CAPTAIN* HAVE TO SAY?

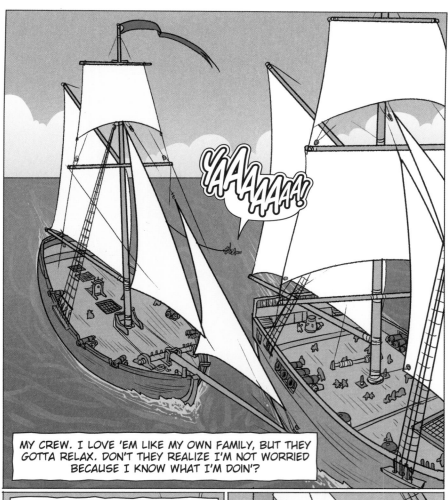

MY CREW. I LOVE 'EM LIKE MY OWN FAMILY, BUT THEY GOTTA RELAX. DON'T THEY REALIZE I'M NOT WORRIED BECAUSE I KNOW WHAT I'M DOIN'?

SARAH. WE'D ALL BE DEAD TEN TIMES OVER WITHOUT HER PATCHIN'.

SOMETIMES SNOOTY LITTLE RICH GIRLS TURN OUT ALL RIGHT. AND I SAY THIS AS A SNOOTY LITTLE RICH GIRL MYSELF.

NOBODY'S A CRACK SHOT LIKE KATI. FRIES UP A MEAN SWEET PLANTAIN, TOO.

FIRING!

DOESN'T TALK MUCH ABOUT WHERE SHE'S FROM. I CAN RELATE.

KA BOOOM!

MIMBA, A NAVIGATOR SO GOOD YOU'D SWEAR IT WERE SUPER-NATURAL. DON'T EVER TELL HER I SAID THAT.

PEW!

WELL, SHE'S A DARN GOOD NAVIGATOR WHEN SHE'S NOT READIN' SOME-WHERE ALONE, THAT IS.

THEY'VE GOT BARRELS ON BOARD...

ZZZP!

LOOKS LIKE OUR FAVORITE.

11

14

23

24

25

26

WELL?

YOU REALLY... THINK WE SHOULD BE GOING BACK OUT THERE?

DOESN'T IT SEEM LIKE... A BAD IDEA?

MIMBA'S RIGHT. IF PIRATES ARE DISAPPEARING MORE FREQUENTLY THAN USUAL—

—AND THEN THERE'S THAT *THING* WE RAN INTO...

HMPH. I AGREE WITH MIMBA, AND YOU KNOW HOW I FEEL ABOUT THAT.

pbth

THE CREW HAS A POINT, ANNE. MAYBE WE SHOULD LAY LOW FOR A BIT?

WE SHOW PEOPLE HOW GOOD THEY COULD HAVE IT, WERE THEY JUST TO GIVE PIRACY A TRY. WE'RE *ROLE MODELS*.

WE SHOW FOLKS THERE'S MORE OUT THERE FOR THEM THAN DOMESTIC SERVITUDE OR A PITTANCE ON A GOVERNMENT SHIP TO JUST END UP WITH A BODY THAT DON'T WORK WELL ANYMORE AND NO WAY TO FEED YOUR FAMILY, AND FOR WHAT?

FOR SOME RICH GOMBEEN IN MERRY OL' ENGLAND TO TAKE WHAT YOU EARNED YOURSELF? FOR SOME BLOWHARD TO SELL YOU LIES ABOUT FREEDOM WHEN THAT "FREEDOM" ISN'T MADE FOR YOU AT ALL?

ARE WE GONNA LET SOME SMOKE AND RUMORS SCARE US OFF THE SEAS? OR ARE WE GONNA GET RIGHT BACK OUT THERE AND BE THE CHAMPIONS OF EQUALITY, AND ALSO MONEY, THAT WE SO SURELY ARE?

... ...

NO WEAPONS DRAWN INSIDE THE CRIMSON TURTLE, ANNE, YOU KNOW THAT.

SO, SHOULD I GO...

OR...?

33

I'LL CROSS AND RETURN TO REPORT ON THE GALLEON'S CREW SIZE. WE APPROACH *SILENTLY*.

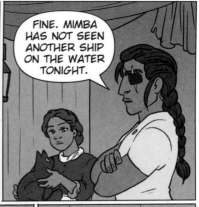

FINE. MIMBA HAS NOT SEEN ANOTHER SHIP ON THE WATER TONIGHT.

DID YOU JUST...STEAL THAT CAT?

HIS NAME IS MACKEREL. AND HE WAS A *STRAY*. BLACK CATS ARE GOOD LUCK ON SHIPS, YOU KNOW. ESPECIALLY ONES WITH EXTRA TOES.

HE HAS EXTRA TOES?!

NO SHIPS ON THE WATER AND A SPANISH GALLEON PASSING THIS CLOSE TO NASSAU...

SOMETHING DOESN'T FEEL RIGHT.

OH, DON'T BE SUCH A *SARAH—*

SHIP HO!

KRMKRMKRM

CCRRRUNCH!

LITTLE GIRLS *AND* SLAVES?

MY. YOU *ARE* ALL VERY FAR FROM HOME.

ANNE. WE HAVE GOT TO GO.

WHAT A DIFFICULT AND MISERABLE LIFE YOU MUST BE LEADING.

WOULDN'T YOU BE SO MUCH HAPPIER IN A NICE WARM BED? WITH SOMEONE TO TAKE CARE OF YOU?

NO. YOU DON'T UNDERSTAND. YOU DON'T—

IT'S ALL RIGHT. I'M HERE TO SHOW YOU THE WAY.

VRRRRM!

43

BRISTOL, ENGLAND. 1708.

WOODES WAS A MERCHANT. ENGLISH, LIKE ME. MARRIED RICH, UNLIKE ME. INHERITED A SHIPPING COMPANY.

HE HAD EVERYTHING GOING FOR HIM. SHOULD HAVE HAD AN EASY LIFE.

BUT THE SEA DOESN'T CARE WHO YOUR FATHER IS OR HOW MUCH MONEY YOU'VE GOT BACK HOME. IT EATS THE WEAK AND THE WEAK-WILLED.

WOODES WAS *BOTH*.

HIS CREWS STARVED. GOT SCURVY. THEIR SHIPS WERE CONSTANTLY UNDER ATTACK.

THEY MUTINIED. WOODES WAS NO MATCH FOR THE PIRATES WHO PLUNDERED THE SEAS.

A TERRIBLE CAPTAIN, THROUGH AND THROUGH.

HE WAS ALMOST FINISHED BY A MUSKET BALL, BUT...

...RUMOR HAS IT HE MADE A DEVIL'S DEAL TO STAY ON THIS EARTH. LET HIM LIVE, AND HE WOULD CLEANSE THE SEAS OF PIRACY, SINGLE-HANDEDLY.

BATAVIAN SURGEONS REMOVED THE BALL FROM HIS JAW.

I THOUGHT IT WAS JUST A STORY. A GHOUL FROM THE SHADOWS TO SCARE GREEN SAILORS ON PIRATE CREWS.

USED TO GIVE ME NIGHTMARES BACK WHEN I FIRST ABANDONED THE DUTCH ARMY FOR PIRACY.

BUT I OUTGREW THEM. OF COURSE, I THOUGHT THEY WERE JUST TALES.

UNTIL NOW.

MY DARLIN'.

HE'S NOT A NIGHTMARE. WE SAW HIM. *AND* HIS SHIP.

DIDN'T LOOK VERY DEVILISH TO ME. LOOKED MORE LIKE NEWCOMEN'S NEW ATMOSPHERIC ENGINE. I WAS JUST READING ABOUT IT—

YES. *MEN* MADE THAT THING.

THERE IS NO DOUBT IN MY MIND.

HELLO?

OH, HERE AGAIN? NOT TO GIVE OUT ABOUT IT, BUT I COULD REALLY DO WITH A CHANGE OF—

WHO-O-O-A!

FWOOSH!

CREW...

GO AWAY, MIMBA.

CREW...!

SIRENS! WAKE UP!

WHASHAPPENIN?

I HAD...

...A VISION.

I DON'T KNOW ABOUT THIS...

BUT I SAW IT. IN A *DREAM.*

THERE ARE WORSE REASONS TO DO THINGS.

MMFMF MFMMMM.

WHAT'S THAT NOW?

SHE SAYS SHE DOESN'T CARE ABOUT YOUR DREAM AND THAT SHE DOESN'T WANT TO DO THIS.

WITH THE WIND, WE SHOULD BE AT NANNY TOWN BY MORNING.

REMIND ME WHY, EXACTLY, WE'RE FOLLOWING THE CAPTAIN'S *DREAMS,* NOW?

BECAUSE MY DREAM IS ALL WE'VE GOT.

I KNOW. I SOUND TWO CARDS SHORT OF A FULL DECK.

BUT MIMBA, I'M NOT TRYIN' TO PUSH YOU HOME BEFORE YOU'RE READY. I SWEAR IT ON THE SEA ITSELF.

YOU KNOW ME! THINGS JUST... WORK OUT!

AND... WHAT ELSE HAVE WE GOT?

OKAY.

IF A DREAM IS WHAT WE HAVE, THEN A DREAM IS WHAT WE HAVE TO FOLLOW.

65

66

WE DON'T KNOW MUCH ABOUT WHY MIMBA LEFT HOME...

SHE'S NOT READY BECAUSE SHE BELIEVES SHE IS NOT READY. YOU SHOULDN'T'VE COME HERE.

MUM...NANNY... PLEASE. WE NEED SOMETHIN' FROM YOU. YOUR HELP.

YOU DON'T NEED A THING FROM ME, FIRE-HEAD.

STAY TONIGHT. I WON'T BE HERE.

WE'RE LIBERATING A PLANTATION. BRINGING PEOPLE THROUGH THE MOUNTAINS TO THEIR NEW HOME, HERE.

BY THE TIME WE'RE BACK, SEE THAT YOU'RE GONE.

PROBABLY MORE KINDNESS THAN I DESERVED, TO BE FAIR.

THANK YOU FOR YOUR HOSPITALITY.

IS THIS SEAT TAKEN?

WAS THAT A JOKE? DID YOU JUST MAKE A JOKE?

WHAT'D YOU WANT?

I AM BRANCHING OUT.

REALLY, NOTHING.

REALLY?

REALLY.

I THOUGHT YOU WERE GOING TO ASK ME TO TALK ABOUT IT.

I HATE "TALK ABOUT IT."

83

QUICK, QUICK, COME INSIDE.

I DIDN'T THINK YOU'D BE BACK FOR WEEKS. YOU KNOW YOUR FATHER IS HOME TODAY!

I KNOW, MAMA. IT'S AN EMERGENCY.

WE'VE BEEN HEARING HORRIBLE THINGS. SHIPS DISAPPEARING... BLACK SMOKE CHOKING THE SKY...I'VE BEEN WORRIED SICK...

I'M SO SORRY, DEAR. I DIDN'T CATCH YOUR NAME.

US PIRATES ARE ALL SO VERY DIFFERENT. DIFFERENT HEIGHTS, COLORS, SIZES. GIRLS, BOYS, NEITHER, BOTH. TALL, SHORT, STRONG, STRONGER.

ANNE BONNY, CAPTAIN OF *LA SIRENE*.

YOU MUST BE ONE OF SARAH'S PIRATE FRIENDS!

...SURE.

BUT THERE'S ONE THING **ALL** PIRATES HAVE IN COMMON.

ALL RIGHT. I'LL BE RIGHT BACK WITH SUPPLIES FOR YOU. STAY QUIET, NOW.

fwoop!

READ—

ALL DUE RESPECT, CAPTAIN, SHUT IT.

YOU WANT ME TO LET THEM GO WHEN IT'S OBVIOUS YOU'VE NEVER EVEN TOLD THEM ABOUT ME? I'M HURT.

WHY WOULD I HAVE?

SAILED ALL THE WAY HERE FROM HOLLAND TOGETHER. FELL IN LOVE. I EVEN FOUGHT A *DUEL* FOR YOU.

YOU DRIP, *I* FOUGHT THAT GUY SO YOU WOULDN'T HAVE TO.

POTATO, POTATO. ALL THAT MATTERS IS THAT YOU RAN LIKE A COWARD WHEN THOSE PIRATES HIT US. *DEFECTED.* WITHOUT SO MUCH AS A GOODBYE.

BUT AFTER ALL THESE YEARS, I NEVER FORGOT YOU. I EVEN KEPT . . .

YOUR TOKEN OF AFFECTION.

MY MOTHER'S KNIFE...

I'VE NEVER FORGOTTEN WHAT YOU DID TO ME. AFTER I KEPT YOUR LITTLE SECRET, TOO. A *GIRL* IN THE NAVY.

NOW, WE TAKE DOWN A PIRATE SHIP, AND IT JUST HAPPENS TO BE YOURS. THAT'S FATE.

AND BEFORE THAT PIRATE-KILLER WE'VE ALL BEEN HEARING ABOUT GOT YOU. THAT WOULD HAVE BEEN A REAL SHAME.

I WAS LUCKY ENOUGH TO FIND YOU. I'M NOT LETTING YOU GO AGAIN. WE'RE GOING BACK DOWN TO THE BRIG.

AND THIS TIME, I'LL USE *CHAINS.*

I'M NOT BLAMING READ FOR THIS LANGER. WE'VE ALL HAD MOMENTARY LAPSES IN JUDGMENT THAT HAVE LED TO, SHALL WE SAY, *REGRETTABLE* RELATIONSHIPS.

I MEAN, LOOK AT ME. I DATED *JACK.*

FINE. Y'GOT US. WE'LL GO QUIET.

GOOD GIRLS.

110

IS THIS SEAT TAKEN?

...NO.

fwump!

SOMETIMES HOME ISN'T A PLACE.

IT'S A PERSON.

116

EVERYBODY ELSE SNOOZIN'?

SARAH'S OUT COLD. KATI AND MIMBA CAME BACK FROM THE SHORE SOAKING WET AND WITH THIS ARROWHEAD.

I DIDN'T ASK.

CUTE.

HOW'RE YOU FEELIN'?

GOOD. FINE. OKAY.

NO, THEY'RE NOT.

NO, I'M NOT. I'M SCARED AND I'M WORRIED AND I KNOW I HAVE TO COME UP WITH A PLAN, BUT I DON'T KNOW HOW.

MY FLOWERIN'... FLOWER, YOU'VE GOT NOTHIN' TO WORRY ABOUT. WE'VE GOT EVERYTHING WE NEED!

NO, WE DON'T. WE HAVE FOUR—OR, I SUPPOSE, WE *THINK* WE DO.

RIGHT. *RIGHT.*

117

MY KNIFE, FOR CUNNING; MIMBA'S POWDER, FOR CONVICTION; KATI'S ARROW, FOR STRENGTH; AND SARAH'S... BALL...THING...FOR KINDNESS? I SUPPOSE?

BUT...WE'RE MISSING SOMETHING OF YOURS. SOMETHING FOR *BRAVERY*.

I'VE BEEN THINKIN' A LOT. I KNOW, I KNOW, TRY NOT TO DIE OF SHOCK.

READ. LOVELIEST OF THE LILIES. COME WITH ME.

THING IS, EVERYONE ELSE HERE HAD TO FACE SOME BIG PART OF THEIR PAST. SOMETHIN' THEY WERE RUNNIN' FROM. *HIDIN'*.

M'DEAR.

PLEASE.

BUT I'M AN OPEN BOOK. EVERYONE KNOWS MY FATHER'S A SLAVE-OWNING PLANTATION RUNNER, ROTTEN TO THE CORE. I'M NOT *HIDIN'* A THING.

DON'T SAY I NEVER TAKE YOU ANYWHERE NICE.

BUT I WAS RUNNIN'. SO FAR AND SO FAST TOWARD DANGER I DIDN'T REALIZE HOW I WAS HURTIN' THE ONES WHO, FOR SOME REASON, DECIDED TO CARE ABOUT ME.

123

LET'S *DO* THIS.

I SPEND A LOT OF TIME THINKIN' ABOUT TOMORROW. HOW PEOPLE ARE GONNA THINK ABOUT US ONCE WE'RE GONE.

I MEAN, *I'M* GONNA LIVE FOREVER. BUT EVERYONE ELSE, Y'KNOW.

THE MEN IN CHARGE, THEY'VE GOT A VESTED INTEREST IN MAKIN' US PIRATES LOOK EVIL. THEY *HAVE* TO.

OTHERWISE, OUR LIFE'S TOO TEMPTING. FAIR PAY AND DEMOCRACY AND EQUALITY? WE'RE *TERRIFYIN'*.

BUT I CAN'T CONTROL TOMORROW.

ALL I CAN CONTROL IS WHAT I DO, RIGHT NOW.

SHE'S NOT GOING TO TELL YOU EXACTLY **WHERE**, OBVIOUSLY.

ALL RIGHT, MY PECULIAR PEONIES, COVE AHOY! ARE YOU READY?

AYE!

fsssh!

128

I'M SORRY, WHAT WERE YOU JUST SAYIN' ABOUT YOUR *RIGHTFUL* PLACE?

YOU ARE *GIRLS* AND *SLAVES*. YOU ARE JUST NOT MADE FOR THIS. IF YOU FACE ME, YOU WILL *DIE*.

IT WOULD BE A WASTE. BUT I *WILL* DO IT.

INSTEAD, WHY DON'T YOU LISTEN TO THOSE WHO KNOW WHAT'S BEST FOR YOU AND TURN YOURSELVES IN PEACEFULLY?

WHAT, *YOU'RE* SUPPOSED TO KNOW WHAT'S BEST FOR *US*—

HA HA HA HA HA HA

WE'LL DO IT!

WE SURRENDER!

JACK?!

AH. OF COURSE. THE *MAN* DISPLAYS SOME SENSE.

LOWER A PLANK AND WE WILL COMMENCE BOARDING. WEAPONS DOWN NOW.

TELL NO TALES: OKAY . . . TELL ONE TALE

Here's the truth: The pirates we're all familiar with from pop culture didn't exist for very long. They only sailed the seas for about a decade, during what we now call the Golden Age of Piracy: 1715 to 1725. And these pirates have a bad reputation today mostly because of what amounted to a large and effective PR campaign against them. Piracy was an exciting alternative for people who were used to being underpaid and mistreated in government navies, an alternative so appealing that it scared the establishment. Those same navies only allowed white men to work aboard their ships, doing difficult, backbreaking labor with little to no benefits. They would leave the navy with life-altering injuries—if they left at all.

Pirate ships, on the other hand, offered much, much more to people in the eighteenth century. These independent vessels prized freedom and teamwork above all. Pirate ships were run like a democracy, where all crewmembers voted for their captain and on difficult decisions, splitting all their bounties equally. They would help out other ships in need and provided disability benefits to injured crew. They admitted women and people of color to their ranks, often people escaping servitude or poverty. They attacked ships carrying enslaved Africans and offered these newly liberated people a life of freedom on the high seas—in fact, formerly enslaved workers made up about a quarter of many pirate crews. Their thing really was stealing from the rich (colonizers and enslavers) and giving to the poor (themselves!). These pirates were viewed as heroes of the common people—and that's what made them so threatening to the establishments of the time. Thus, the coordinated campaign to make people think pirates were bad when, actually, that couldn't have been further from the truth.

Anne Bonny and Mary Read were two of these real-life pirates. Bonny was born in Ireland in 1698 and immigrated to South Carolina with her parents as a little girl. Her father owned a plantation, but Bonny—said to be "robust" with a "fierce and courageous temper"—ran away from home at twenty, landing in New Providence, an island in the Bahamas. There, she met Captain Jack Rackham, also known as "Calico Jack" for his bright patterned clothes. He told Bonny about his wild adventures as a pirate, and Bonny joined up right away. Pants on and sword buckled, it was on this ship that Bonny ran into another pants-wearing pirate: Mary Read. Read had been born in London, England, in 1695, and grew up mostly pretending to be a boy to earn money for an impoverished single mother. Read was "bold and strong" and at thirteen signed up to be a sailor, first for the British navy and then for a Dutch merchant's ship. That Dutch ship was attacked by pirates—and Read quickly decided to switch sides in the hopes of a better life.

Bonny "took a particular liking to" Read immediately, at first assuming that Read was a boy. When the two revealed to each other the truth about themselves, they developed an instant "intimacy." Together with Captain Jack, Bonny and Read sailed the Caribbean, stealing from fishing and merchant ships around Cuba, Haiti, Bermuda, and Jamaica. It was well-known that Bonny and Read were the boldest members of Jack's crew, "both very profligate, cursing, and swearing much, and ready and willing to do any thing on board." Though they often wore dresses, Bonny and Read also ". . . wore men's jackets, and long trousers, and handkerchiefs tied about their heads, and each of them had a machete and pistol in their hands." They sailed the southern seas, and they defied class and gender norms in the process.

The rest of Anne's crew was inspired by people and places in and around the Golden Age of Piracy. Sarah Walker was a real person; her father, Captain Thomas Walker, made himself "the de facto governor of New Providence" in the Bahamas using an expired contract. But New Providence was a pirate haven, and Captain Walker had no real authority. Historical accounts describe Sarah as biracial; her mother may have been a formerly enslaved worker or a freeborn woman of color. We don't know much about her personality, and she probably wasn't a medical student, but that's where the magic of fiction comes in!

Kati wasn't inspired by any particular person, but rather by a people: the Miskitu, a Central American society formed by the local indigenous population and formerly enslaved Africans along the Caribbean coastline of what is now Honduras and Nicaragua. This once-fertile region for hunting and agriculture remains home to the Miskitu people, though their lands and way of life are under threat. We've messed with historical timelines a bit for the sake of our book, here—the Miskitu maintained independence until 1894 but did face many battles with Spanish colonizers throughout the eighteenth century. The *grisi siknis* Kati experiences is a real affliction, mostly found in teenaged Miskitu girls and is still studied by doctors and researchers today.

Mimba, too, is an invention—but Nanny and her Maroons are not. Enslaved Africans in Jamaica escaped their British captors and fled into the mountains, forming their own, independent community with other free people of color and indigenous people. They were called the Windward Maroons, probably from the Spanish word for fugitive. We adjusted timelines here again, a little, but the Maroons were led by Queen Nanny, a title of respect, from 1728 to 1740. This middle-aged woman held many roles: She was a warrior, general, and military strategist who executed many raids against the British and successfully defended her community from attack, freeing more than a thousand enslaved workers despite being vastly outnumbered. She was responsible for maintaining her peoples' traditional culture, music, and legends from Africa. And she was a spiritual priestess with supernatural powers, an Obeah woman who gained her power from her ancestors. After years of fighting (including Nanny Town's destruction), Nanny secured a treaty that guaranteed the Maroons' freedom.

And Woodes Rogers was real, too: a failed English captain with a chip on his shoulder against pirates. He was generally the worst at being a captain. His crews mutinied and got scurvy; they sued him for not paying wages, and he was forced into bankruptcy; he took a musketball to the face . . . But Rogers's stories did contribute to the best history book we have about pirates, the book from which we get most of our pirate tales, *A*

A GENERAL

HISTORY

OF THE

Robberies and Murders

Of the moſt notorious

PYRATES,

AND ALSO

Their *Policies, Diſcipline* and *Government,*

From their firſt Riſe and Settlement in the Iſland
of *Providence,* in 1717, to the preſent Year 1724.

WITH

The remarkable Actions and Adventures of the two Female Pyrates, *Mary Read* and *Anne Bonny.*

General History of the Robberies and Murders of the Most Notorious Pyrates by someone writing under the pseudonym Captain Charles Johnson in 1724. And it's from Johnson's book that we get one of our records of Bonny and Read's time on the seas, including the only known illustration we have of them, standing on a beach, surrounded by palm trees, swords out. They look happy, they're together, and they look free. And that's Bonny and Read, to me.

Even though we know so much about Anne Bonny, Mary Read, and the people they may have interacted with during their time at sea, I always felt like we didn't know *enough*. I wanted to know what it would be like if Bonny had broken off from Rackham and gotten her own ship, if she and Read really had been a couple, if they'd picked up any other awesome folks while out plundering on the water. I've always been fascinated by their true story . . . but what if there was just a little *more*? That's the question Kendra and I asked ourselves when we sat down to come up with the plot and characters of *Tell No Tales*. So much of history is written by the victors—and, usually, the victors have mostly looked the same (straight, white, dudes, etc.). Kendra and I decided we wanted to reclaim some of our lost history—the history of women and non-binary and queer folks that *must* have existed, but has been hidden or kept quiet for so long that it may never be recovered. So instead of waiting . . . we decided to create our own.

We hope you enjoyed our interpretation of Bonny and Read and their crew on the southern seas, and we hope you'll come back for more. We all tell our own tales. What's yours?

NOTES

154 "robust": Johnson, Charles. *A General History of the Pyrates, from Their First Rise and Settlement in the Island of Providence, to the Present Time*, 171.

154–155 "fierce and courageous temper": Johnson, Charles, 171.

155 "bold and strong": Johnson, Charles, 158.

155 "took a particular liking to", "intimacy": Johnson, Charles, 162.

155 "both very profligate . . . willing to do any thing on board" and "wore men's jackets . . . each of them had a machete and pistol in their hands": *The Tryals of Captain John Rackam and other Pirates*, 18.

155 "the de facto governor of New Providence": Bartlinksi, Jim. "A Brief Account of Sarah Walker Fairfax, the Mother of Sarah Fairfax Carlyle," 2.

SELECTED BIBLIOGRAPHY

Appleby, John C. "Women and Piracy in Ireland: From Gráinne O'Malley to Anne Bonny." In *Bandits at Sea: A Pirates Reader*, edited by C. R. Pennell, 283–298. New York: New York University Press, 2001.

Bartlinski, Jim. "A Brief Account of Sarah Walker Fairfax, the Mother of Sarah Fairfax Carlyle." *Carlyle House Docent Dispatch*, June 2009.

Bethell, A. Talbot. *Early Settlers of the Bahamas and Colonists of North America*. Phoenix, AZ: Heritage, 2008.

Brathwaite, Edward Kamau. *Nanny, Sam Sharpe, and the Struggle for People's Liberation*. Kingston, Jamaica: Agency for Public Information, 1977.

"By his Excellency Woodes Rogers; Governour of New-Providence, &c. A Proclamation." *Boston Gazette*, 10-17 October 1720.

Campbell, Mavis Christine. *The Maroons of Jamaica, 1655–1796: A History of Resistance, Collaboration & Betrayal*. Granby, MA: Bergin & Garvey, 1988.

Canfield, Rob. "Something's Mizzen: Anne Bonny, Mary Read, 'Polly,' and Female Counter-Roles on the Imperialist Stage." *South Atlantic Review* 66, no. 2 (Spring 2001): 45–63.

Carey, Bev. *The Maroon Story: The Authentic and Original History of the Maroons in the History of Jamaica, 1490–1880*. St. Andrew, Jamaica: Agouti Press, 1997.

Cary, Wilson Miles. *Sally Cary: A Long Hidden Romance of Washington's Life*. New York: The De Vinne Press, 1916.

Cordingly, David. "Bonny, Anne (1698–1782)." In *Oxford Dictionary of National Biography*, edited by Sir David Cannadine. Oxford: Oxford University Press, 2008.

———. *Life Among the Pirates: The Romance and the Reality*. Abacus, 1996.

———. "Read, Mary (c. 1695–1721)." In *Oxford Dictionary of National Biography*, edited by Sir David Cannadine. Oxford: Oxford University Press, 2008.

———. *Under the Black Flag: The Romance and the Reality of Life Among the Pirates*. New York: Random House, 2006.

Cueto, Gail A. "Nanny of the Maroons." In *Notable Caribbeans and Caribbean Americans: A Biographical Dictionary*, edited by Serafín Méndez-Méndez and Gail A. Cueto, 324–26. Westport, CT: Greenwood Press, 2003.

Cwik, Christian. "The Africanization of Amerindians in the Greater Caribbean: The Wayuu and Miskito, Fifteenth to Eighteenth Centuries." *Dimensions of African and Other Diasporas*, edited by Franklin W. Knight and Ruth Iyob, 83–104. Kingston, Jamaica: University Press of the West Indies, 2014.

Duncombe, Laura Sook. *Pirate Women: The Princesses, Prostitutes, and Privateers Who Ruled the Seven Seas*. Chicago: Chicago Review Press, 2017.

Fallon, Joseph E. "Miskitu History." *Miskitu Nation Foundation*. savemnf.org/miskitu-history/

Frankel, Estelle Valerie. *Women in Game of Thrones: Power, Conformity, and Resistance*. Jefferson, NC: MacFarland, 2014.

Goldsmith, Oliver. "Essay X: Female Warriors." *The Miscellaneous Works of Oliver Goldsmith, with an Account of his Life and Writings*, Volume 4, edited by Washington Irvine, Esq, 314–19. Paris: Baudry's European Library, 1837.

Gottlieb, Karla. *The Mother of Us All: A History of Queen Nanny, Leader of the Windward Jamaican Maroons*. Trenton, NJ: Africa World Press, 2000.

Herlihy, Laura Hobson. "Matrifocality and Women's Power on the Miskito Coast." *Ethnology* 46, no. 2 (Spring 2007): 133–149.

———. *The Mermaid and the Lobster Diver: Gender, Sexuality, and Money on the Miskito Coast*. Albuqueque: University of New Mexico Press, 2012.

Johnson, Charles. *A General History of the Pyrates*. London: T. Warner, 1724.

Little, Benerson. *The Golden Age of Piracy: The Truth Behind Pirate Myths*. New York: Skyhorse, 2016.

Meyer, W. R., revised by Randolph Cock. "Rackam, John [nicknamed Calico Jack] (d. 1720)." In *Oxford Dictionary of National Biography*, edited by Sir David Cannadine. Oxford: Oxford University Press, 2008.

Munson, James Donald. *Col. John Carlyle, Gent., 1720–1780: A true and just account of the man and his house*. Alexandria: Northern Virginia Regional Park Authority, 1986.

Noveck, Daniel. "Class, Culture, and the Miskito Indians: A Historical Perspective." *Dialectical Anthropology* 13 (March 1988): 17–29.

O'Driscoll, Sally. "The Pirate's Breasts: Criminal Women and the Meanings of the Body." *The Eighteenth Century* 53, no. 3 (September 2012): 357–79.

Rediker, Marcus. "Liberty beneath the Jolly Roger: The Lives of Anne Bonny and Mary Read, Pirates." In *Iron Men, Wooden Women: Gender and Seafaring in the Atlantic World, 1700–1920*, edited by Margaret S. Creighton and Lisa Norling, 1–33. Baltimore, MD: Johns Hopkins University Press, 1996.

Riley, Sandra. *Homeward Bound: A History of the Bahama Islands to 1850 with a Definitive Study of Abaco in the American Loyalist Plantation Period*. Miami, FL: Riley Hall, 2000.

Salmonson, Jessica Amanda. *The Encyclopedia of Amazons: Women Warriors from Antiquity to the Modern Era*. New York: Paragon House, 1991.

Sharp, Anne Wallace. *Daring Pirate Women*. Minneapolis, MN: Lerner Publications Company, 2002.

Sharpe, Jenny. *Ghosts of Slavery A Literary Archaeology of Black Women's Lives*. Minneapolis, MN: University of Minnesota Press, 2002.

Sivapragasam, Michael. "After the Treaties: A Social, Economic and Demographic History of Maroon Society in Jamaica, 1739–1842." PhD dissertation, University of Southampton, 2018.

Sjoholm, Barbara. *The Pirate Queen: In Search of Grace O'Malley and Other Legendary Women of the Sea*. Berkeley, CA: Seal Press, 2004.

Thornton, John K. "The Zambos and the Transformation of the Miskitu Kingdom, 1636–1740." *Hispanic American Historical Review* 97, no. 1 (February 2017): 1–28.

Tryals of Captain John Rackam and other Pirates, The. Pamphlet, printed by Robert Baldwin, 1721.

Twaska, Josephenie Hendy Hebbert. *Yapti Tasbia: The Miskitu Motherland*. Self-published, Lulu, 2014.

Vasquez, Dr. Jorge J. *Miskitos: A Brief Profile of an Indomitable Nation*. Converse, TX: Instituto de Formación de Líderes Espirituales, 2019.

Wedel, Johan. "Involuntary mass spirit possession among the Miskitu." *Anthropology & Medicine* 19, no .3 (July 2012): 303–14.

"Preface." In *Calendar of State Papers Colonial, America and West Indies: Volume 28, 1714–1715*, edited by Cecil Headlam, v–xlvi. London: His Majesty's Stationery Office, 1928. *British History Online*. british-history .ac.uk/cal-state-papers/colonial/america-west-indies /vol28/v-xlvi.

Williams, Caroline A. "Living Between Empires: Diplomacy and Politics in the Late Eighteenth-Century Mosquitia." *The Americas* 70, no. 2 (October 2013): 237–68.

Woodward, Colin. *The Republic of Pirates: Being the True and Surprising Story of the Caribbean Pirates and the Man Who Brought Them Down*. Orlando, FL: Harcourt, 2007.

Yolen, Jane. *Sea Queens: Women Pirates Around the World*. Watertown, MA: Charlesbridge, 2008.